Poster Removed 1/6

A GREYHOUND'S TALE
Running for Glory, Walking for Home

written by
CRAIG PIERCE

illustrated by
TONY SANTIAGO

HC STORM STUDENTS—
MANY HAPPY TALES!
12/2008

American Dog® and American Dog Tales® are registered trademarks of Ideate Prairie, LLC.
For more information about this book and upcoming titles, please see www.americandogtales.com

IDEATE PRAIRIE, LLC
Published by Ideate Prairie
PO Box 65, Genoa, Illinois 60135

10 9 8 7 6 5 4 3 2 1

A Greyhound's Tale: Running for Glory, Walking for Home
Second Edition, 2006

Text copyright © Craig Pierce, 2004
Illustrations copyright © Tony Santiago, 2004

Library of Congress Control Number: 2004098346

ISBN: 0-9762564-2-8
13-Digit ISBN: 978-0-9762564-2-7

Printed in China

In memory of Hilly Farmer and Gator Slide.

With special thanks to family and friends for your support and encouragement. - CP

For Roxanne, Fabi, Mateo and Angel. Thank you. - TS

reyhounds are graceful lean and quick.
Watching them run provides quite a kick.

Folks come from miles just to see them race,
as they chase along at an amazing pace.

And among all greyhounds, none ranked greater
than the champ people knew simply as Gator.

When the gates flew open he'd start with a burst,
pass all the dogs and finish in first.

Gator won more races than any other hound.
You could barely see him with his trophies all around!

Indeed, stories were told and tall tales spun
about Gator the Greyhound...how fast he could run!

But this story is different and a wee bit amazing.
It's more about his friends and less about his racing.

It all began one day just before a race.
The sky looked as gloomy as Gator's sad face.

He gazed about from crate to crate.
Something was missing. He didn't feel great.

His friends were leaving. Each one by one.
And they never came back to enjoy another run.

Gator asked, "Where's Jake, Kudos and Quest?
What happened to Binky, Betty and the rest?"

"They're gone," sighed Hilly, Gator's one remaining friend.
"I'm afraid their racing days have come to an end."

"But why?" asked Gator. "Racing is fun.
There's nothing more enjoyable under the sun."

Hilly looked at Gator with an amused grin.
"Of course you have fun, because you always win."

"Besides," said Hilly, "Our friends are just fine.
Their lives are even better than yours and mine."

"They've each been adopted into wonderful homes.
They spend their days napping and chewing on bones.

"They live in houses the size of a hundred dog crates.
And sometimes lick people food right from the plates!

"And when they have an urge to run real hard,
they just step outside to a big fenced yard.

"Their new families are great. That's what I've heard.
Yes, our friends are fine. You can trust my word."

Gator's eyes opened wide. His brown ears perked up.
"So why can't a champ be such a lucky pup?"

"I'm sorry," sighed Hilly. "You're just too fast.
The dogs that get adopted are those that finish last."

"Hilly," Gator said, "I know your words are true.
If I want to get adopted, I know just what to do."

Later that evening at quarter past eight,
Gator waited patiently behind the starting gate.

Suddenly, the gates opened! The race began in a flash.
Eight speeding dogs in a long, oval dash!

True to his nature Gator charged from the back.
In the blink of an eye he was leading the pack!

Then something happened. Something quite stunning.
Gator simply decided it was time to stop running.

He skidded to a stop. While the crowd stared in shock
at Gator the champ standing still as a rock.

And when the other hounds had finally passed,
Gator walked to the finish line happy he was last!

Trainer Hank looked puzzled as you'd imagine.
"Gator, you've never lost in such a fashion."

"Well," Hank said, "You can't win every time.
Perhaps you need a break and then you'll be fine."

Three days passed. Gator raced again.
With the same results - no desire to win.

Quick as lightning he'd start every race.
Then he'd stop in the middle and stroll to last place.

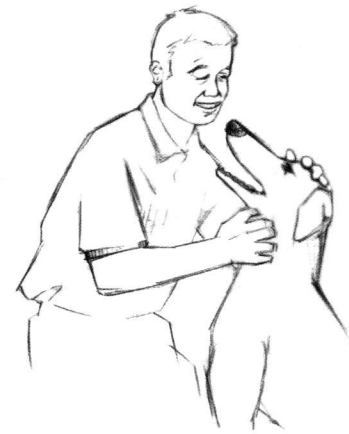

Trainer Hank told Gator, "Your racing days are through.
You've been a great champ and now I want to help you.

"I have found you a home not far from here.
You'll get bones and treats as big as a pig's ear.

"And blankets thick and fluffy, as if made for royalty.
Indeed you'll be the king of your new family."

Gator's tail began wagging. His eyes brightened too.
A new life was beginning...for his wish had come true.

**G**ator's day finally came to meet his new family.
There was Mom and Dad and a boy named Stanley.

Up in the van and away they did go
to a place in the country Gator didn't know.

Finally they arrived at Gator's new home.
He could see his fenced yard and how far he could roam!

And there was his house along the horizon.
But it was those stairs Gator had his eyes on.

He'd seen them before but never so tall.
Would he make it to the top or would he just fall?

Stanley bounded up the stairs and called out with pride,
"C'mon up Gator! I'll show you inside."

Gator paused and stared at the steps so high.
He swallowed hard and gave it a try.

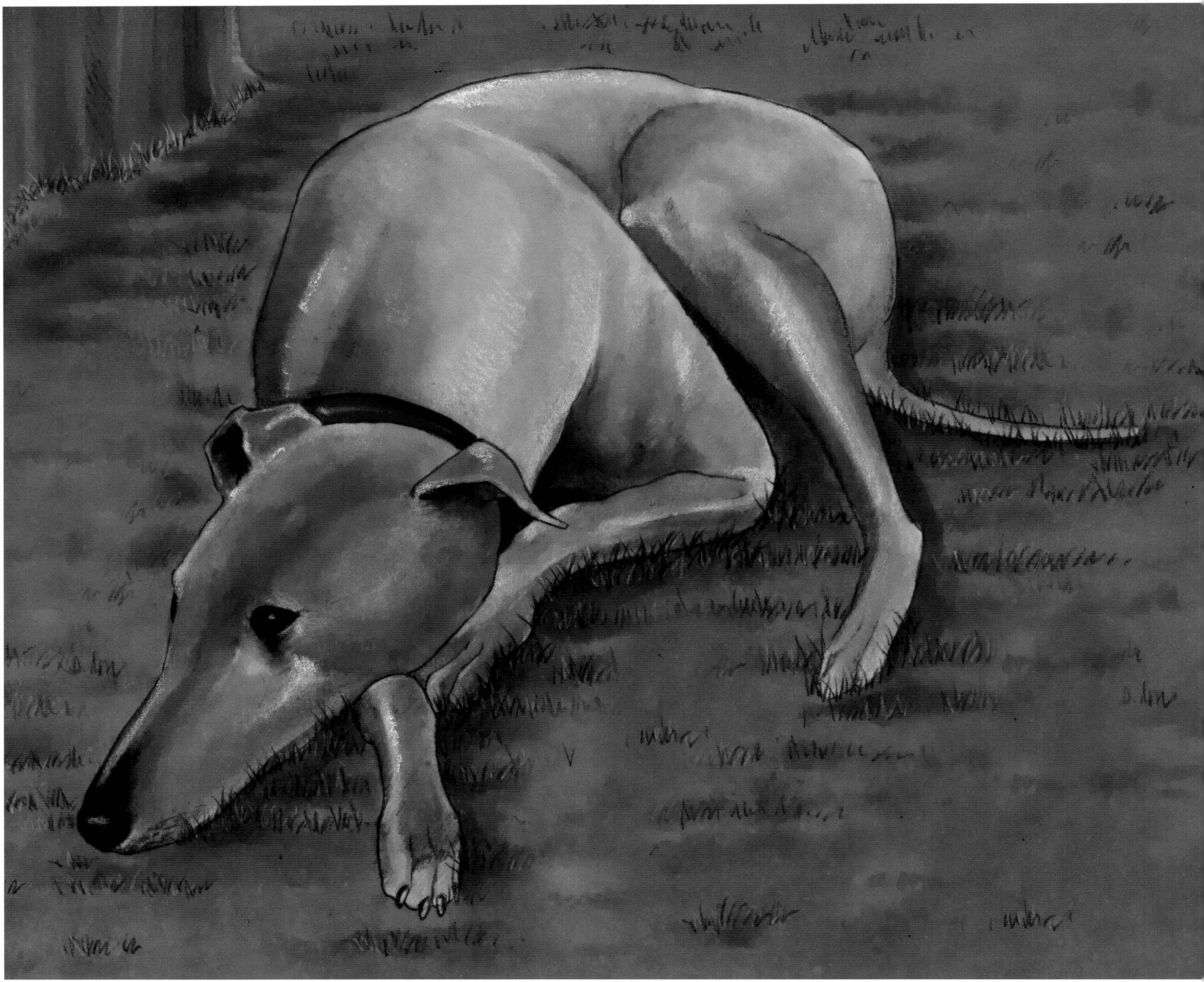

Slooooowly, Gator began up step one, two and three.
Then he scrambled back down and laid under a tree!

He thought, *I'm comfortable here lying on the ground.*
Those stairs weren't built for this long-legged hound.

"Come here and help Gator," Dad called to his son.
"He's never climbed stairs, they must not look fun."

They prodded. They pushed. They tried to be gentle.
But Gator wouldn't budge. He proved quite a handful.

Mom had an idea as she held out a treat.
Then, even the stairs couldn't stop Gator's feet!

He followed her right up with his nose fully twitchin'.
Before Gator knew it he was there in the kitchen.

"You're a good boy!" Stanley told Gator.
"I knew you'd make it sooner or later."

Then out of nowhere rang a high-pitched sound.
It frightened Gator and made his heart pound.

"Don't worry," said Stanley. "It's just the phone.
I guess you never heard one in your old home."

Stanley answered the phone and shouted, "Hello Uncle Syd!
Come meet the dog we just adopted."

The doorbell rang a half hour later.
It was old Uncle Syd, but where was Gator?

He was in Stanley's room staring in the mirror.
The closer he looked, the "other" dog came nearer.

Gator sniffed and snorted and pressed nose to nose.
But whenever he stopped the "other" dog froze!

Stanley tapped the mirror to end the confusion.
"Gator, that's not a dog, it's just an illusion."

Gator looked baffled. He didn't understand.
This new life was stranger than he had first planned.

Then Uncle Syd threw a toy he brought from the store.
But Gator wasn't experienced with such a slick, tile floor.

Gator's heart and his legs told him to chase.
The slippery floor put an end to his race.

He looked as silly as an octopus unfolding a beach chair!
His legs spinning wildly without going anywhere.

Gator crashed with a thud. The poor little guy.
He didn't feel like a champ. He wanted to cry.

He scrambled to his feet and slinked down the hall.
"I'm sorry," groaned Syd, "For making you fall."

Stanley approached Gator, soothed him with a hug.
"From now on boy we'll only play on the rug."

Mom scratched Gator gently behind his ears.
It felt so good but he still had his fears.

Gator thought about things that turned his stomach sour.
The stairs, phone, floor and mirror...yikes, it's only been an hour!

Well the days finally passed. Gator learned to adjust.
By the end of the week the family had Gator's trust.

They gave him a bed, the fluffiest he'd seen.
They fed him big meals with cookies in between!

And mornings were great as Stanley awoke at dawn.
Time for a walk after a stretch and a yawn.

Stanley walked Gator on a leash as he should
while delivering newspapers to the neighborhood.

The same thing happened day after day.
First a walk, then a nap, then time for more play.

But one morning Gator woke up and noticed something wrong.
He looked around for Stanley and Stanley was gone.

Gator searched room to room through lonesome, amber eyes.
In a "Sad Face Contest" he'd surely win the prize.

"Come here," called Mom, and Gator arrived in a hurry.
"Dad and Stan will be back. There's no need to worry."

"Sorry, I must also leave." Mom started to explain.
"I'm going to the city now. I've got to catch the train."

Gator's tail, once wagging, now drooped down to the floor.
When he was left home alone life was just a bore.

Gator laid on his bed though he was truly quite restless.
He waited for his family. The hours felt endless.

He thought about the race track and his days as a champion.
But he mostly thought about Hilly, his true greyhound companion.

I wonder if she's happy or if she's all alone.
I'd call her right this minute if I could only dial a phone.

I sure miss little Hilly, my friend through thin and thick.
Whenever I think about her I feel a bit homesick.

Loneliness made Gator drowsy. He quickly began to snore.
But soon he was awakened by the creaking of a door.

Stanley and Dad walked in, their faces fully beaming.
Dad said, "Wake up, Gator! Or you'll think you're dreaming."

"Gator, we have great news!" added young Stanley.
"We brought home an addition to our growing family!"

Gator looked out the window and couldn't believe his eyes.
It was his old friend Hilly - what a tremendous surprise!

Gator started to dance. He leaped and jumped around.
His tail swirled crazily. His paws barely touched the ground.

Gator bounded out the door and Hilly became excited.
There was good 'ol Gator! She was visibly delighted.

She spun herself in circles as Gator raced down the stairs.
They both were truly happy, free from all their cares.

And do you know they played, romped, wrestled and chased?
Like two frisky puppies, not a minute went to waste.

Stanley joined them too. They all frolicked in the lawn.
Thanks to his friends, Gator's loneliness was gone.

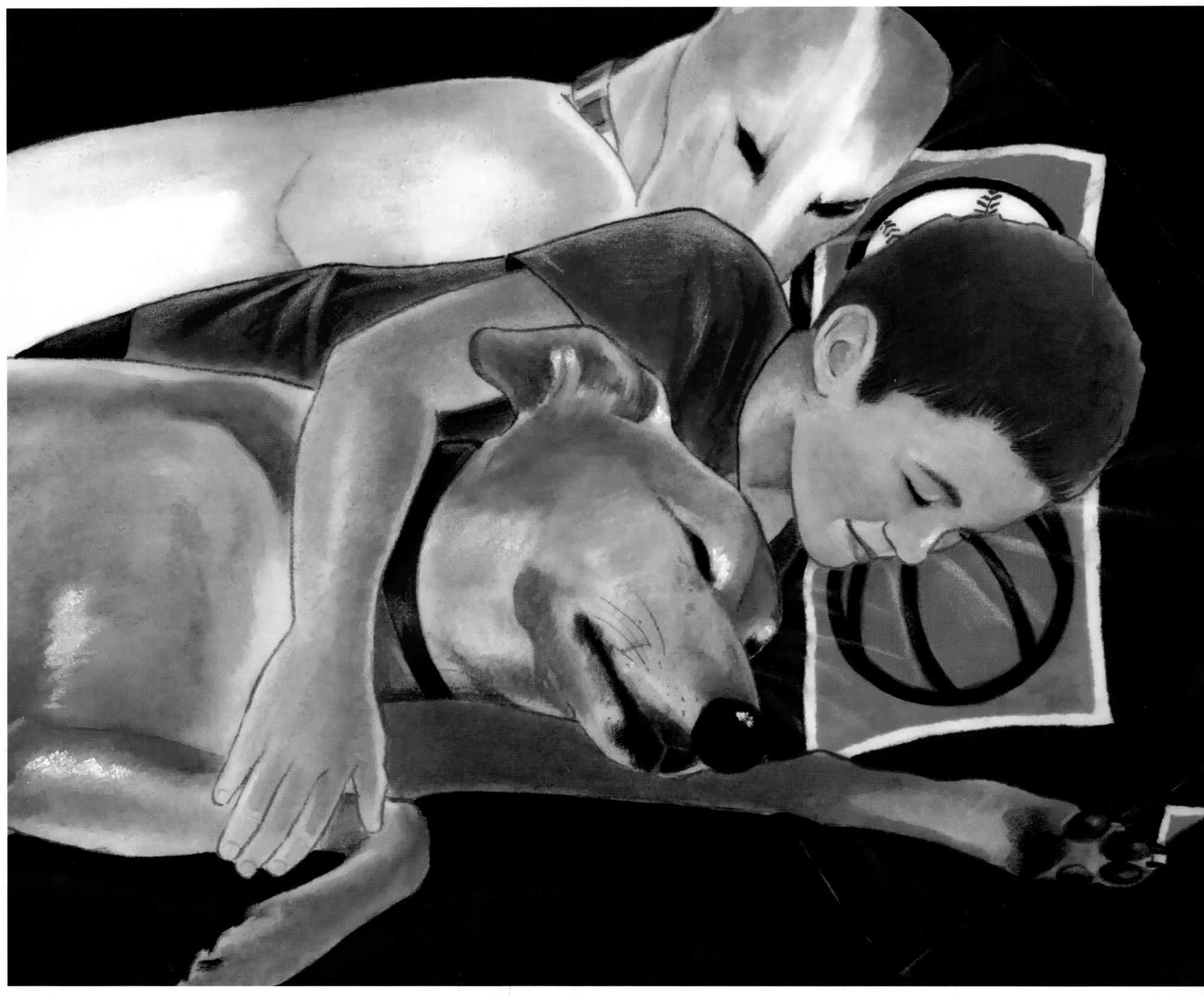

Finally at sunset, the three began to tire.
The day that started so low couldn't finish any higher.

Mom called, "Come on in!" So up the stairs they went.
Three exhausted pals, each feeling quite content.

Gator tugged at his blanket and tried to spread it out.
He made room for everyone - a gentleman no doubt!

It didn't take too long for each to fall asleep.
They laid down side by side, and never made a peep.

Gator smiled as he dreamed along side his two best friends.
His life could not be better. And that's how this story ends.

From Racing Dog to Couch Potato

Gator talks about Adoption

"Usually we're about three years old when we're 'retired' from racing. Race tracks often find us a new home, but most times we're sent to a greyhound adoption group.
A group of volunteers meet us for our first day off the track. They give us a bath, a pedicure and a full inspection. It's like a doggie day spa! Before we get too adjusted to this pampered life, we're sent to the vet. They say we're getting 'fixed' so there aren't too many puppies. Yeowww! Next we head to a foster home and learn about stairs, mirrors and fuzzy little critters called cats. We stay with the foster home until they find us a good permanent home. Oh wait…Stanley is calling. Gotta go!"

Do you know…

Greyhounds are considered one of the oldest breeds - dating back thousands of years!

✓Ancient Greeks worshipped greyhounds
✓It's the only dog mentioned in the Bible
✓Cleopatra and Egyptian Pharaohs owned greyhounds

As part of the sight hound family, Greyhounds can see up to a half-mile away.

Greyhounds are typically quiet and mellow - they rarely bark and have been called the "gentle giant" among dogs.

Greyhounds reach speeds of 40 miles per hour. Only the cheetah is faster.

A daily walk or a quick run is all the exercise a greyhound needs. They are remarkably lazy with short bursts of energy. Many sleep 18 hours a day!

Because of their chasing instinct and sheer speed, greyhounds must be in a fenced yard or on a leash when outside.

Retired greyhounds make excellent service dogs - their calm nature is a hit with nursing home residents and other groups.

American Dog® supports greyhound adoption.

For more information please see our website:

www.americandogtales.com